This book belongs to

_____

For Mom —C. H.

For Vera —D. M.

Library of Congress Cataloging-in-Publication Data available.

ISBN 978-1-4521-6650-6

Manufactured in China.

MIX
Paper from
responsible sources
FSC™ C020056

Design by Jennifer Tolo Pierce.

Typeset in Miyares Drawn.

The illustrations in this book were rendered in graphite, gouache, and digital collage.

10 9 8 7 6 5 4 3 2

Chronicle Books LLC
680 Second Street
San Francisco, California 94107

Chronicle Books—we see things differently. Become part of our community at
www.chroniclekids.com.

BiG
AND
SMALL
AND
IN-BETWEEN *

Carter Higgins

Daniel Miyares

chronicle books · san francisco

the SUN and its SHINE

when it asks you to rise

the DONUT

that your brother got
because you picked last
and only got the hole

a PILE of LEAVES

after they've all been raked

and before you

jump

the **TROPHY** you got for the jump-rope contest

because your feet remembered the pattern

those KIDS on the playground
when you want to use the seesaw
and so you swing instead

the ELEPHANT'S TEA PARTY
and his stack of jam sandwiches
and the chip in his teacup

a MESS

even the accident kind

when there aren't enough rags

to clean it up

how much BRAVERY it takes to jump into the deep end

without the floaty things on your arms

how QUIET it gets

when it's your turn onstage

and you're not sure

about your talent

the way the MOON looks
if you use a telescope
and spin the fuzziness out

a BEAR

and her MAMA

and her POP

and the HUGS they probably give

each other

the HOLE when you are done
with the digging

the CASTLE when it's finished

the way the OCEAN feels when it
stands in front of you

2

the DIRT that knows

the promise underneath

and the sunshine that's above

the TEETER-TOTTER

not when it's up

or when it's down

but when two smiles meet in the middle

your TOOTH

when it wiggles and waggles
but isn't all the way in

or all the way out

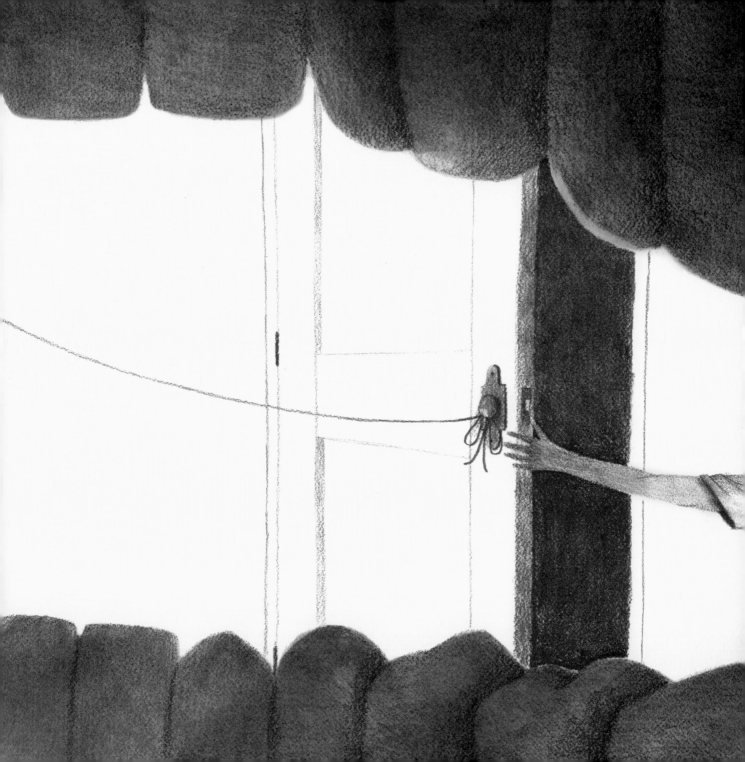

what you are

on your HALF BIRTHDAY

not even or odd

the leftover BALLOONS

that are losing their oomph

but not all the way droopy

a BOAT below the sky

and above the swell

the CATERPILLAR

that once was an egg

but will fly away soon

a handful of NICKELS

that fell out of a pocket

and got smushed in the sofa

the WATER that got dirty
because it cleaned your brushes
so you could make this

those cozy SOCKS

that keep your feet warm

and your shoes less smelly

and the CHOCOLATE

and the other

graham cracker

when the MARSHMALLOW

gets gooey and sticks to

the graham cracker

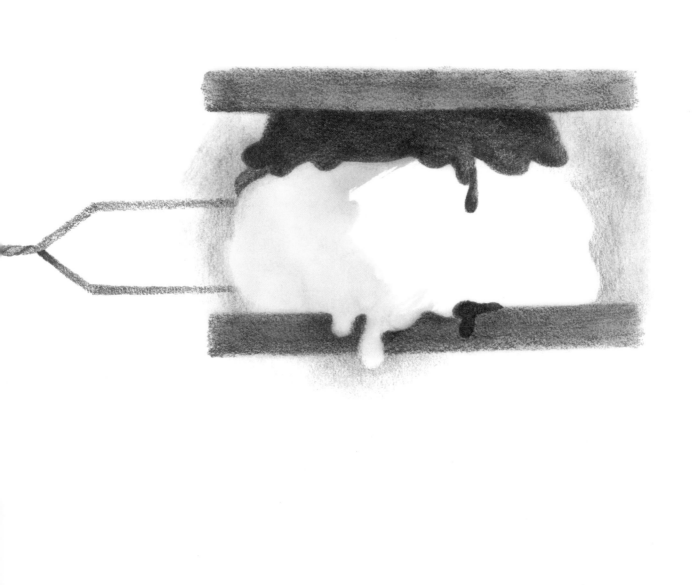

the STARS

that make a picture

in the middle of the night

when the **outside** and the **inside** of the hole

are about the same

and the **tide** pulls your castle back to sea

and the **OCEAN** floats between you

and another world

the baby blue PROMISE in a robin's nest
and the BIRD beginning to sing

and the WORM

who wished he hadn't been seen

the PLIP of a raindrop

and the PUDDLE where it falls

for a butterfly to sip

the SEED
that was
stuck
in the
soil

and the
CARROT
that
didn't
want
to grow

and his

shy

green

CROWN

that tried

anyway

a SNAIL and her HOME and the road she has traveled

WHAT'S LEFT of your fort
after your mom says
to clean up those pillows

the GOLDFISH you love
and his EYES that tell you
he's a good listener

the MOUSE'S TEA PARTY
and her swiss cheese SANDWICHES
and the CHIP in her teacup

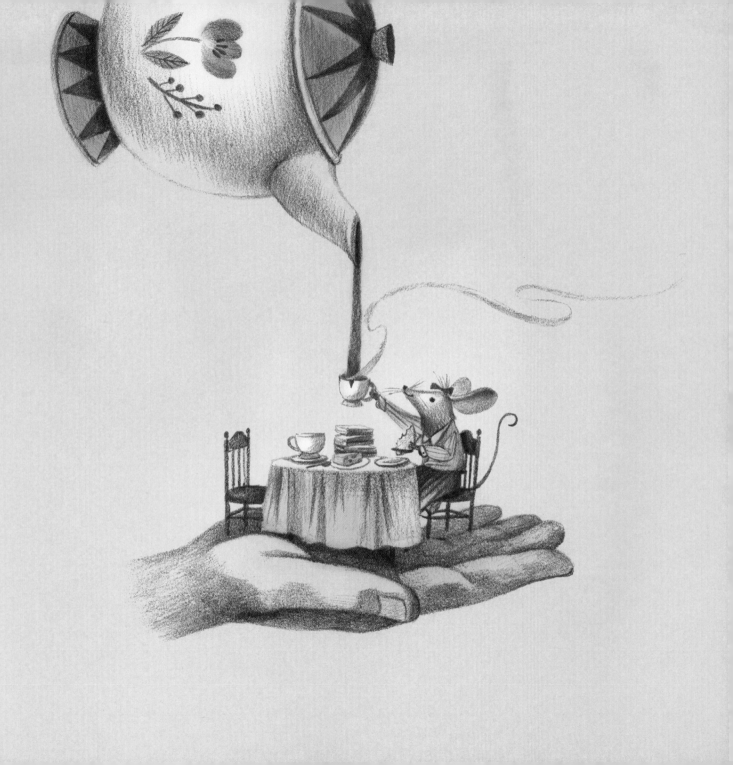

the SUN right before it slips away
when it is going

going

gone

the BRIGHT LIGHTS

that stick around

after your sparkler stops fizzing

the **WISHES** you leave for the tooth fairy

and **THE ONE** you trade

for a handful of coins

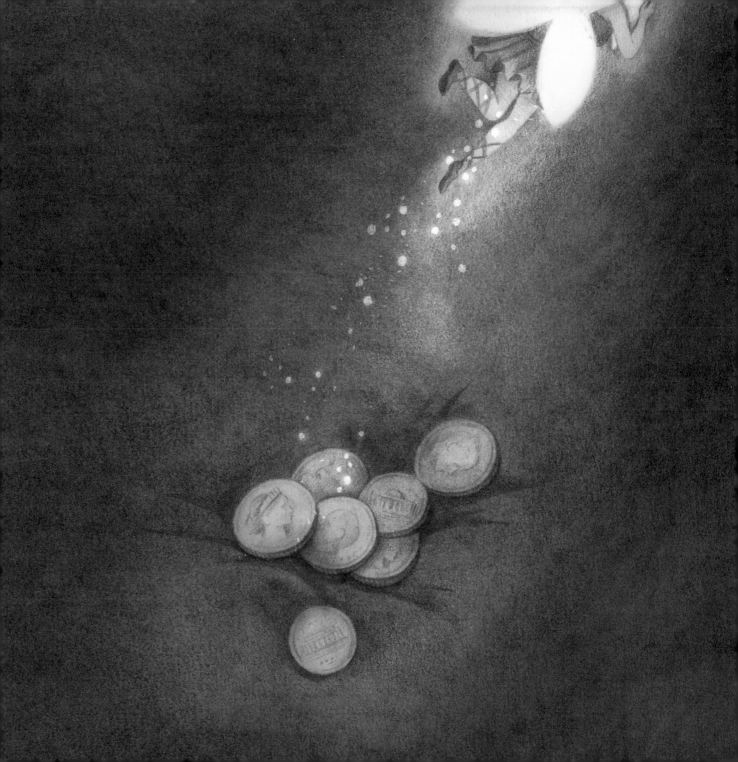

the SLIVER of moon

that sneaks in through the window

and the barely-there BREEZE

and the DREAM DUST it brings

the **HOLE** when you start to dig

the **CASTLE** when you start to build

the WAY
YOU FEEL

when

you stand

in front

of the ocean

4

everything

the bluest SKY

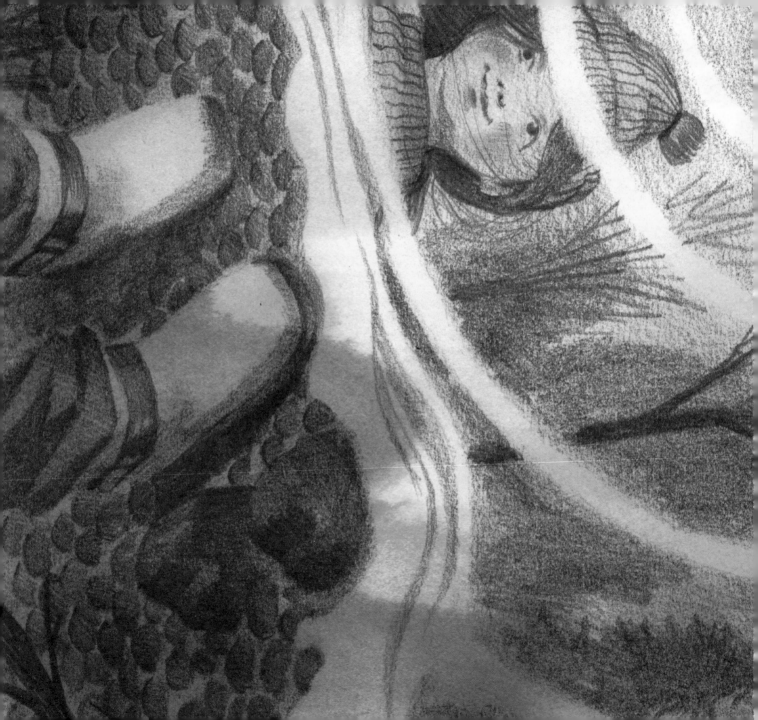

in the middle of it all

and you

the bittiest BUG

CARTER HIGGINS is the author of *Bikes for Sale* and *Everything You Need for a Treehouse* and the author and illustrator of *Circle Under Berry*, among other books. She lives in Los Angeles, California.

DANIEL MIYARES is a critically acclaimed picture book author and illustrator. He lives with his family and dog, Violet, in Lenexa, Kansas.